MALUS THE MONSTER

in

'Beastly'

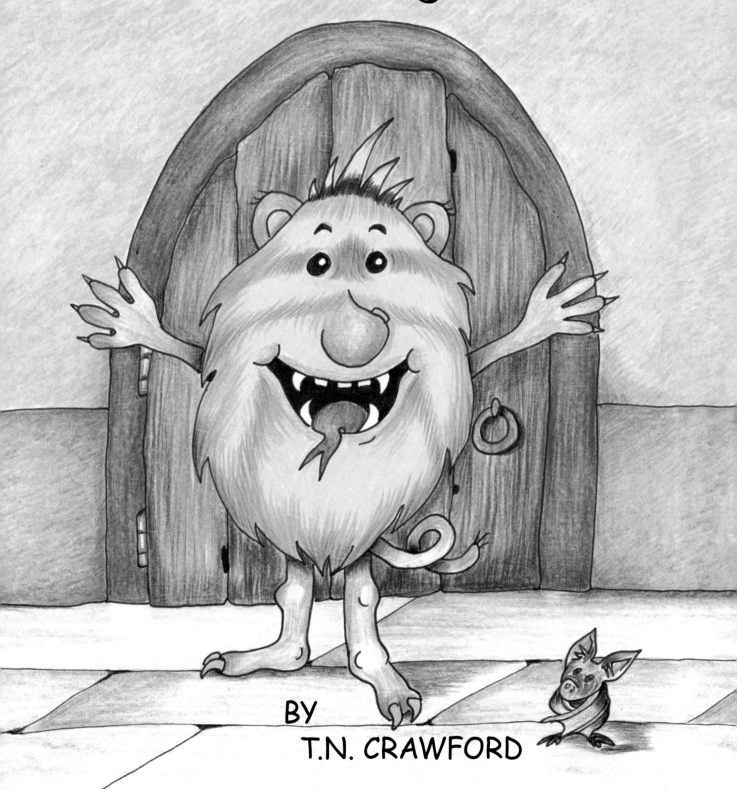

BY
T.N. CRAWFORD

AuthorHouse™ UK
1663 Liberty Drive
Bloomington, IN 47403 USA
www.authorhouse.co.uk
UK TFN: 0800 0148641 (Toll Free inside the UK)
UK Local: 02036 956322 (+44 20 3695 6322 from outside the UK)

ISBN: 979-8-8230-8776-6 (sc)
       979-8-8230-8778-0 (hc)
       979-8-8230-8777-3 (e)

Library of Congress Control Number: 2024910488

Print information available on the last page.

Published by AuthorHouse 05/24/2024

MALUS THE MONSTER

in

'Beastly'

An idle crow makes a crude complaint,
with Harvest gone, barren soils acquaint,
crisping leaves, rust and gold,
there's magic to behold,
as traces of Summer become faint.

Down a narrow lane, with trees lining,

is a cottage with windows shining,

for they're made to reflect,

take effect and protect

against those who are undermining.

4

Frae is a good witch with second sight,
the seventh born on a Wolf Moon's night,
her daughter is unique,
for Nicole there's mystique,
living with a bat,crow and a sprite!

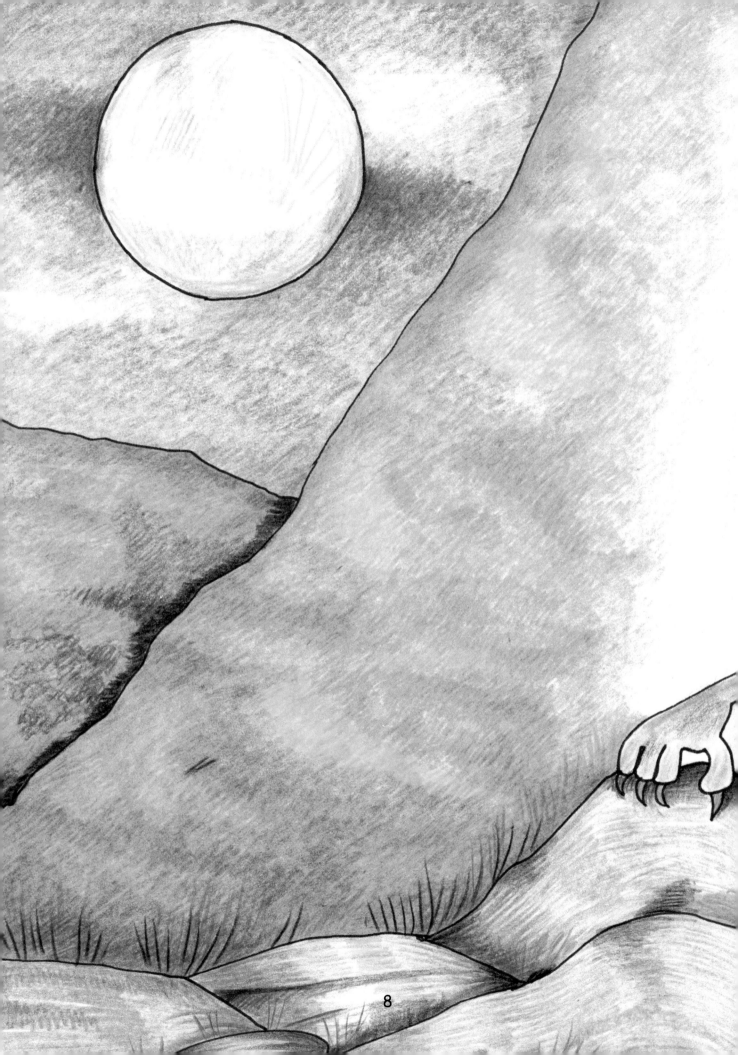

8

On a Hunter's Moon, a monster did crawl,
through the torrents of a waterfall,
from ear to ear it smiled,
ravenous for a child,
searching for a naughty one that's small.

Frae's raucous crow set off the alarm,
as Malus the monster intends harm,
panicking with concern,
when she didn't return,
Malus would feel her protective charm.

The log rafters moaned with her torment,
eerie sobs, through oaken doorway went,
casting a shielding spell,
so Nicole will stay well,
by snatching her, Malus was hell bent.

The bright little Sprite said "Use the Quill !",
writing down the truth was her best skill,
"Weakness will be paper!"
"But him do not vapour!"
she was determined with wish and will!

Spellbinding Malus from eating meat,
and bewitching him, so to defeat,
with her wand set to stun,
"You return my loved one!"
with the bat's help, the spell was complete!

The inky crow was about to speak,
as the weathered door began to creak,
Malus peered through the crack,
he had brought Nicole back,
delighted they both let out a shriek!

The vegan monster became a friend,

had a bath, so as not to offend,

his manner was now mild,

never taking a child,

as monsters queued, he started a trend!

Witches and monsters were in accord,
no longer part of a frightening horde,
judge not what you see,
a changed beast you'll agree,
having met them, they're simply adored!

Printed in the United States
by Baker & Taylor Publisher Services